Rude Stories

By Jan Andrews
Illustrations by Francis Blake

Tundra Books

Text copyright © 2010 by Jan Andrews
Illustrations copyright © 2010 by Francis Blake
Published in Canada by Tundra Books,
75 Sherbourne Street, Toronto, Ontario M5A 2P9

Published in the United States by Tundra Books of Northern New York,
P.O. Box 1030, Plattsburgh, New York 12901

Library of Congress Control Number: 2009938093

Library and Archives Canada Cataloguing in Publication

Andrews, Jan, 1942-
          Rude stories / by Jan Andrews ; illustrations by Francis Blake.
Short stories.

ISBN 978-0-88776-921-4

I. Blake, Francis II. Title.

PS8551.N37R83 2010   jC813'.54   C2009-905856-1

We acknowledge the financial support of the Government of Canada through the Book Publishing
Industry Development Program (BPIDP) and that of the Government of Ontario through the
Ontario Media Development Corporation's Ontario Book Initiative. We further acknowledge the
support of the Canada Council for the Arts and the Ontario Arts Council for our publishing program.

ONTARIO ARTS COUNCIL
CONSEIL DES ARTS DE L'ONTARIO

Design: Terri Nimmo

Printed and bound in China

1 2 3 4 5 6   15 14 13 12 11 10

A rude story you're looking for, is it?
I don't think you're going to want me.
I don't shoot my peas at my brother —
At least not when others can see.

I may rant and rage in the mornings.
I may rant and rage at the night.
In between that I'm truly quite lovely.
It's my granny that's sometimes a fright.

ONE

MR. MOSQUITO

Once! That's how all good stories start now, isn't it?
Once, in the long ago times, when donkeys
walked on their hind legs and pigs went around with
forks stuck into their backsides all ready to be turned into your
dinner. Once, in those times, there was this creature who seemed
like he was trying out for the rudest being in all the world.

His name was Mr. Mosquito. You can guess why *that* was,
of course.

Oh, he was an awful thing. He never had a kind word to say
to anybody. He never did anything you might call nice. Just about
every day there was someone knocking on the door of his home
to complain about him. The worst of it was, he thought he was
the strongest, smartest, handsomest being on all the face of all the
earth. He couldn't bear it that anyone might be better than him.
He just could not.

There were all these travelers going around in those days.
One of them showed up in the village where Mr. Mosquito

lived. The traveler told everyone how in a deep, dark forest in a far-off land there was an ancient castle. In that castle there was a certain Ms. Candle. She'd been there forever, so he said. Men had come and men had gone, but no one had been able to put out Ms. Candle's flame.

When Mr. Mosquito heard this, he leaped up in excitement. He flexed the muscles on his little mosquito arms. He yelled out about how he'd be able to do what no one else had, and then he went home to his mother.

"You get me together some food," he ordered her. "You make sure it's a lot, and you wrap it up tight."

His mother did as she was told. She seemed to think she had to. She worked all night, cooking meat and potatoes and baking bread for him. She put the food into a bag, although there was hardly anything left for her or for his father. There was almost nothing in the house.

Mr. Mosquito didn't thank her; he just set out. He walked and he walked and he walked. He was ready to walk forever almost, he was so certain he'd be the mighty one.

At last he saw the castle ahead of him. The door had a big black knocker on it. Mr. Mosquito didn't use it. He went right on in.

"Ms. Candle," he called out.

He got no answer.

"You must come to greet me!" he shouted.

Still nothing happened.

"I shall have to find you then," he proclaimed.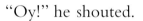

He walked down a long, long hallway. He came to a room with a high, high ceiling. Ms. Candle sat in the middle of the room, perched in a candleholder with a tall, tall stem.

Mr. Mosquito let out a cough to announce his presence to her. Ms. Candle took no notice. He didn't like that; he didn't like it at all. He gave her a whistle, one of those nasty ones.

"Oy!" he shouted.

Her flame didn't even flicker.

"I am here to put an end to your eternal brightness," he insisted. She was ever so calm and still.

"I am Mr. Mosquito and you are going to get it," he threatened.

If anything, her lovely yellow flame rose higher. That made him mad. He went toward her. He swelled up his cheeks to blow her out. He huffed and he puffed. Her flame bent sideways.

"Aha!" he cried in triumph.

Her flame stood up.

"I shall punch you," he bellowed. He didn't waste any time. He drew back his fist and slammed it into her. The only thing was, he hadn't given any thought to how her flame might be hot. His hand got burned. It shriveled up to nothing. It was turned into this blackened kind of a stump on the end of his arm.

He went home a whole lot more quickly than he'd come. He ran all the way, shrieking, "I'm hurt. I'm hurt. I'm hurt."

His mother took one look. She knew there was nothing she could do. She brought Mr. Mosquito to his father. His father knew he couldn't do anything either. They went with Mr. Mosquito to the doctor.

The doctor saw what had happened. He knew there was no fixing it.

"You'll have to have a new hand. I'll have to graft it onto you," he declared.

"Will the new hand be better than the old one?" Mr. Mosquito asked him.

"It might and it might not," said the doctor. "I don't have any mosquito hands in stock at the moment. I only have chicken hands, or maybe I should say chicken feet."

A chicken foot seemed better than nothing, so Mr. Mosquito let the doctor stitch it on. You'd think that would have put a stop to his nonsense, but it didn't. The chicken foot was so big it filled him with new boldness. Off he went to visit Ms. Candle again.

He walked that long distance. He went through that big door. He begged and he pleaded and he threatened. He said Ms. Candle needed a good slapping. He reached out and took a swipe at her. Another hand got burned. It was a crisp, I'm telling you.

He knew what to do now though, didn't he? He went back to the doctor and had a chicken foot stitched there as well. Somehow that made him even more determined. Back he went to the castle for another try.

Did he think how Ms. Candle had never done any harm to anyone? Did he think how beautiful her light was? He didn't.

Before he was finished, he had six chicken feet, four chicken wings, and a chicken rump.

After the twelfth visit, he had to get a chicken head stitched on. That's when he finally put an end to the whole business. Besides, he was too busy being famous, strutting down the streets with people looking at him, telling everyone he was something of a miracle. Girls were swooning over him even. He liked that. He liked it a great deal.

Still, he wasn't above thinking he might also like a change. He was out for a little stroll one day. He saw a man swimming in the river. The man was skinny-dipping. He had nothing on. He was in distress.

"A thief has stolen my clothes from where I left them," he

MR. MOSQUITO

called out. He was weeping almost. "I have nothing to put on myself. How am I going to get out of here? People will recognize me. What am I going to do?"

Turned out, he was the local mayor, a person of importance. Mr. Mosquito saw his chance.

"Say I lent you my head," he suggested. "No one would recognize you then."

"Would you do that?" the mayor asked.

"I would do it willingly," said Mr. Mosquito. "I would need something to put in its place, of course. I would suggest that you might lend me yours."

The mayor was out of the water in an instant. He came clambering up the riverbank. Still, he did have some wits about him.

"Our arrangement is only until I get home, isn't it?" he asked.

"Certainly, certainly," said Mr. Mosquito.

(You'll notice Mr. Mosquito was talking a bit differently now.)

The mayor took the chicken head. He took it gladly. He gave Mr. Mosquito the one that was his. He started to say how grateful he was.

"Do not thank me too soon," Mr. Mosquito told him.

"Too soon?" asked the mayor.

"I believe we are being hasty," said Mr. Mosquito. "I believe you might be known by your feet."

"Might I exchange those also?" asked the mayor. "It will be the same as with the head. It will be until I get home. It will be no longer."

"But," said Mr. Mosquito, "we cannot be too careful."

"Too careful?"

"There is the matter of your hands and your arms."

The mayor was looking less like himself every minute.

"There is also your rump to attend to."

The mayor didn't know whether to talk or cluck.

"We will meet up later," Mr. Mosquito told him.

He left the mayor standing there with his chicken mouth hanging open. Mr. Mosquito went to the mayor's house. He took on all the mayor's duties. He dressed himself up in the mayor's finery. He found out the mayor was about to be married to this pretty young lady. He decided he'd marry her instead.

The wedding was a grand affair. There was food set out on groaning tables, there was music, and there was dancing. Everyone came from miles around. Mr. Mosquito was having a high old time when the real mayor showed up. Of course, the real mayor wanted his body back. He wanted his bride as well.

Who was going to believe someone with a chicken head, chicken wings, and chicken legs? Mr. Mosquito certainly wasn't going to bother with him. Why would he even think of doing that?

The mayor was desperate. He went round talking to everyone.

"I'm not really what I look like," he kept saying.

People were fed up with him. It seemed as if he was going to spoil the evening.

"Off with you or you'll find yourself stuffed, roasted, and being served for supper," Mr. Mosquito told him.

Finally, the mayor left. You'd think that would be enough.

You'd think Mr. Mosquito would be satisfied, but he wasn't. He had the village boys run after the mayor and pelt him with rotten tomatoes and kick him on his chicken rump.

I wish I could tell you Mr. Mosquito got what he deserved at some point, but I'm afraid I have no proof of that. Truth to tell, he might be the mayor of the very place you're living in. He might now. Who can say?

A rude story, you tell me you're wanting?
Well, surely I can't be the one.
I don't often steal all the raisins
When we have sticky cinnamon buns.

I don't drink my pop all that quickly,
I don't make it come down my nose –
Unless there's an aunt come to visit,
The one with the frills and the bows.

THE SKELETON
IN THE ROCKING CHAIR

R ude. Rude. Rude.

What I'm going to tell next is a story about a woman who was so rude she wouldn't even stay in her grave the way she was supposed to. She wouldn't even accept the right and proper rules for dying. For her, there was no lying quiet and unmoving in her coffin beneath the earth, with her eyes and her mouth shut still and tight.

This was once too, of course. It was a different once though. It was the once when monkeys hadn't even begun to grow their tails yet, when worms came wriggling up out of the dirt to greet you in the morning, and when earwigs and slugs and snails and all the world's creepy crawlies could be counted on to say hello.

I don't think she was related to Mr. Mosquito, but she might have been. Folks from all over came to attend her funeral. They all knew she was so nasty the cat wouldn't even scratch her for fear it got blood poisoning. They all wanted to be certain she was safely in her grave. They watched the coffin being lowered. They went home satisfied.

Her poor old husband went home too. He'd hardly got himself indoors. He hadn't even had time to make himself a cup of tea. There she came, bold as brass, walking into the kitchen in all her burial finery. She settled herself in the rocking chair. (It was the only comfortable chair in the house, I might add. Her husband had been looking forward to a turn in it for a change.)

Rock, rock, rock she went, and with every rock there was a squeak.

The afternoon passed by and then the evening. Didn't matter how many times her husband told her she ought not to be there. Didn't matter how often he reminded her she'd better be moving along.

"I might be dead, but I'm not finished," she kept saying. "I'll sit here forever, if I like."

Night fell. He went to bed without her.

He heard the rocking and squeaking first thing when he woke up. It was still going on. Down the stairs he came. He'd never been able to leave her when she was alive, now had he? He certainly couldn't leave her when she was dead.

His life now, though — it was a great deal worse than it had been. Apart from anything else, it seemed she'd forgotten his name. If she'd just gone on calling him a blathering idiot instead of Harry the way she'd done before, he wouldn't have minded, but she couldn't seem to stop at that any longer.

"You old clinchpoop," she'd say to him.

"You cockamamy flapdoodler."

"You shivering, withering cesspit."

"You ninny-pated crow foot."

On and on and on.

She was after him for the house cleaning. "Do you think because I'm dead I can't see there's a hair in that corner?"

She was after him for the cooking. "Do you think because I'm dead I don't need to eat?"

She was after him for the dishes. "Do you think because I'm dead I didn't notice you only rinsed that pot twice over?"

He was at his wit's end. It was true he could see she was shrinking. First her clothes were hanging off her, then her skin. Then she didn't have any flesh on her. There were just her bones.

But that was almost worse still.

Rock, rock, rock, rock.

"You crab-faced bandicoot."

Her jaw was going at him.

"You grub-toed homunculus."

"You lug-loaf milksop, galoot of a lummox."

Rock, rock, rock, rock. Squeak, squeak, squeak, squeak. Rattle, rattle, rattle went her bones.

No one came to visit, of course. Why would they? Who wants to be sitting down for a nice, polite conversation with the remains of a corpse?

When Harry heard a knock he was happy. He was even more happy when he saw a fiddler at the door. He thought he might like some music to lighten his load a little.

"Come in," he said. "Come in."

The fiddler got a surprise when he saw Harry's wife in the rocking chair, but he didn't say anything. He reckoned he'd better not. Harry offered the fiddler a bite of food and a sup. For some reason, Harry's wife was silent – except for the rocking and the squeaking and the rattling, of course. Maybe she was sulking. I don't know.

"Could you give us a tune?" asked Harry.

The fiddler gave the wife a look. It was cold and dark outside.

He wasn't ready to be going on yet. He took his fiddle out of its case.

"A jig or a reel?" he asked Harry.

Harry thought for a moment. "A jig," he said at last.

"A jig it is," said the fiddler.

Out came his bow. Up went the fiddle under his chin. The notes of his music went soaring through the kitchen. Something weird happened. Harry's wife's face (well, what was left of it) lit up.

"Time for some fun," she sang out.

Harry wasn't expecting that. Still, he wasn't about to interfere

with her enjoyment. After all, she was snapping her bony fingers. She was tapping her bony toes.

"Fun, fun, fun, fun," she was crying.

Not only that, now she was up and dancing. Harry had never seen anything like it. She was moving in perfect time.

The fiddler came to the end of his tune.

"Should I keep on playing?" he demanded.

"Did I tell you to stop?" roared Harry's wife.

Harry gave him a nod. The fiddler started in on a reel.

"Do you have anything faster?" Harry's wife asked.

"Much, much faster," answered the fiddler.

"Fun, fun, fun, fun," Harry's wife yelled out.

The fiddler played "The Olympic Reel." He played it as fast as he could. Harry's wife was flinging her arms and legs about by that time. She was still in perfect rhythm, but she was looking like a fir tree in a gale.

"Why aren't you dancing too, you grumptious, old stick shank?" she asked Harry.

Harry couldn't even reply. Bits of her had started flying off in all directions. He had his work cut out for him, sweeping them up. Fingers and toes, ribs and collarbones – they were all over.

"Faster," she told the fiddler. "Faster."

A hip bone came Harry's way. He caught it.

"Fun, fun, fun, fun."

Her spine had given up on the whole business. There was only her head now, moving and floating and swaying through the air.

"Fun, fun . . . ."

Wouldn't you know it? Her jaw had dropped off. It had fallen to the floor.

"I reckon maybe that's enough for her," Harry said.

He was right too. Her head couldn't go on by itself much longer. It drifted under the kitchen table. There it stayed.

"I expect you need a rest," said Harry to the fiddler.

The fiddler was sweating. He put down his bow.

"Would you like me to cook you a big dinner?" Harry asked him. "Would you like me to give you a bed?"

"It'd be grand," said the fiddler.

"I'm a good cook. I've had lots of practice," said Harry. "I'll just finish cleaning up."

He put his wife's bones outside in a pile. He and the fiddler had a lovely meal together. They even had some wine.

"You're welcome back any time you want to come stay here," Harry told the fiddler in the morning.

The fiddler said he might do that, he just might. He went on his way.

Harry was left to his own devices. He looked out the window. He saw the sun was shining. He saw it was a beautiful spring day. He took that rocking chair to the bottom of the garden and he burned it. He let the flames rise high. He went out and bought himself a chair that was softer, a chair he could laze in. He spent quite a while lazing and taking pleasure in things from that time on.

I'm not too keen on story morals, but I reckon there's got to be one for this. If you ask me, I'd say it has to do with how behaving yourself is something you should consider whether you're alive or dead.

Still, you might think Harry's wife was really just waiting around until she could go out happy. There's at least a fair chance you might be right.

Oh rudity, screwdity, scrabble.
Can I help it if on certain days
My stomach is given to rumbling,
My mind's in a kind of a haze?

My fingers just reach up to scratch at
What happens to be on my head?
My eyeballs get bigger and rounder
And fill my poor daddy with dread?

THREE

A RED ONE, A GREEN ONE, AND A BLUE ONE

Have you heard about Ti-Jean? Have you? He wasn't rude at all. That doesn't mean rude things didn't happen to him. They happened quite often, in fact. Especially if you count rude as . . .

I don't think I'll tell you about that though.

I think I'll just tell you when the once of Ti-Jean's story was. It was a good once, no doubt about it. It was the once when cows hadn't even learned to moo yet, cats couldn't meow, and stores hadn't been invented. If you wanted a garden fork or a refrigerator or a set of men's long underwear, you had to pick it off a tree.

The big thing to know about Ti-Jean is that he was a dreamer, and what he dreamed about mostly was girls. The trouble was, he didn't know any. His family was poor. They lived on a little farm, but it never seemed to produce much. They had to sell everything they grew to keep the landlord from turning them out. This year, too, it had been worse than ever. They were looking forward to a winter of eating nothing but turnips.

No girls in sight!

Then, they had a surprise. They got up one morning to find the pig had given birth to three lovely piglets. They weren't just ordinary piglets either. There was a red one, there was a green one, and there was a blue one.

Ti-Jean's father rubbed his hands together. "Maybe this'll save us," he said.

From that day onward, the whole family did everything they could to keep those piglets strong. They wrapped them in blankets at night; they went out into

the forest to gather acorns for pig feed during the day. They kept the sty so clean you could've eaten out of the trough.

Time came when those piglets were the right age for taking to the market to sell. Ti-Jean volunteered. He thought the market might be the place to go for meeting some you-know-whos.

"You must get a good price," his father told him.

Ti-Jean promised he would. He picked up the little red piglet and put it in a sack. Off he went, whistling away to himself with the sack over his shoulder, dreaming his dreams. Some of those dreams were about what the family was going to get to eat through the winter – stews and steaks and roasts. But mostly those dreams were about soft, smooth cheeks and lovely dancing eyes.

He hadn't gone very far when he heard a carriage coming behind him. It was big and it was drawn by six white horses. To his amazement, instead of going past him, it stopped. A princess stepped out. She was smiling and she was beautiful. Her cheeks! They looked softer than he could have imagined; they were smoother. Her eyes! They were – they were dancing!

"I'd like to see what you are carrying in your sack," the princess told him.

Ti-Jean opened the sack at once.

"I have never seen a red piglet before," said the princess.

"I'm taking it to the market to sell," Ti-Jean replied.

"The market is a long way to walk," said the princess.

Ti-Jean nodded in agreement.

"You could give the piglet to me," said the princess.

The turnips flashed through Ti-Jean's mind.

"If you would give the piglet to me, I would take you into my carriage. I would show you something you have never seen before."

The turnips flew off from Ti-Jean's thoughts, as if they'd never been. Before he knew it, he was passing the little red piglet in the sack over to the coachman. He was politely helping the princess up the carriage steps. He was climbing in himself. He was closing the carriage curtains, just as she'd told him. He was kneeling beside her.

"Are you ready?" the princess asked him.

"I am ready," Ti-Jean whispered.

"So!" said the princess.

She lifted up her long gown. She lifted up her long petticoats. She showed Ti-Jean her ankle. Ti-Jean saw a mark there. The mark was in the shape of the sun. The princess let her gown and her petticoats fall into place again.

"Is that all?" Ti-Jean asked her.

"It is plenty," said the princess. "You must step down now. I have matters to attend to. I must be on my way."

Ti-Jean stepped down. He stood there, watching the carriage and the princess disappearing and thinking about what his mother and his father were going to say to him. He wasn't dreaming about that.

His father told him he was stupid and a whole lot of things that were worse. His mother set him into eating turnips and only turnips that very night.

"I'll go off again in the morning. I'll take the green piglet," Ti-Jean told them.

"Will you take it to the market?" asked his father.

"For sure. And I'll come back with a lot of money," he declared.

A RED ONE, A GREEN ONE, AND A BLUE ONE

Ti-Jean fell asleep that night dreaming money and princess dreams, although I think he dreamed about the princess more.

Still, he wanted to be careful. He had turnips for breakfast, just to remind himself of what his purpose was.

He set out right enough. He put the green piglet in another sack. He swung that sack over his shoulder. Of course, though, he was hoping. He couldn't help himself. You can guess what he was hoping for.

Sure enough, there was the carriage coming behind him. There were the six white horses. There was the princess, stepping out.

"What have you got for me to look at today?" she asked him.

There can't be any harm in her just looking, Ti-Jean thought. He opened the sack.

"A green piglet today. Isn't that amazing?" the princess burst out.

"It is amazing," Ti-Jean replied. "It might even be worth gold."

"But it is so very sweet," said the princess. "And since I already have a red one . . ."

Ti-Jean tried to bring the taste of turnips to his mouth. Suddenly turnips didn't seem so bad.

"I could save you the walk. You could give me the green piglet also," said the princess.

"I'm not sure it's a good idea," Ti-Jean managed to get out.

"But if you would give it to me, I would take you into my carriage and show you something you have never seen before."

What is so terrible about turnips at every meal? Ti-Jean wondered. *What is so very wrong with that?*

He gave the green piglet in the sack to the coachman. He helped the princess into the carriage. He closed the carriage curtains. He knelt down beside her.

The princess lifted up her long gown. She lifted up her long petticoats. She raised them to her knee. Ti-Jean saw there was another mark. This mark looked like the moon.

"The sun and the moon," he murmured.

"Yes," said the princess.

"Is that all?" asked Ti-Jean as she lowered her petticoats and her gown once more.

"It is plenty," said the princess. "I must be on my way."

Ti-Jean stepped out of the carriage. He waited by the roadside, waving good-bye. He went home very slowly. His parents were not pleased to see him. They were not pleased at all. His father took out a stick and threatened to beat him. His mother gave him double turnips. She made him clean his plate.

"Give me one more chance," Ti-Jean begged them.

"The blue piglet is all that is left to us," said his father.

"Yes," said Ti-Jean. "I know."

He went to bed early. He tried very hard to dream only of pigs and sales. Morning came. He got up before it was light. He didn't eat any breakfast. He didn't want to waste any time.

He put the blue piglet in a sack. He swung that sack over his shoulder. He kept his eyes fixed on the road ahead. The carriage with the white horses thundered up behind him, just as it had the other days. The princess stepped out of it. She smiled at him.

"Do you have another piglet for me to see?" she asked.

"I do," said Ti-Jean, "But . . . "

"But surely I may look at it."

There is *no harm in looking,* Ti-Jean thought.

"A blue piglet this time." The princess was so excited.

"I have to go to . . . "

"Three colored piglets would be perfect. A red one, a green one, and a blue one."

"My parents will be eating . . . "

"If you would give me the blue one, I would take you into my carriage and I would show you something no man has seen – not ever."

"No man?"

Ti-Jean was putting the blue piglet, in its sack, into the hands of the coachman. He was helping the princess into the carriage. He was climbing up himself. He was closing the curtains. He was kneeling beside her.

She was lifting up her long gown. She was lifting up her long petticoats. She was raising them to her thigh. Ti-Jean saw there was another mark. This mark looked like the stars.

"The sun and the moon and the stars," he murmured.

"The sun and the moon and the stars," said the princess. She let her gown and her petticoats fall again. She settled them around her.

"Is that all?" Ti-Jean asked her.

"It is all," she said.

Ti-Jean got back down onto the road. The coachman whipped the six white horses. The carriage moved off. Ti-Jean watched and watched until all he could see was a cloud of dust. When even the dust was gone, he started walking home once more. His father and his mother were so angry they wouldn't even speak to him. That was the worst of all. Ti-Jean busied himself with clearing out the root cellar and putting turnips into it. His back ached with the work.

Winter came. It was a cold one, cold and long. Every day, when he and his father and his mother sat down to eat, Ti-Jean thought about what an idiot he'd been. He also

thought about the princess. He was still a dreamer. Nothing could alter that. Nothing could change how beautiful she'd seemed to him.

Winter passed. Spring flowers started blooming. One day, a herald rode up to the farm. He was dressed all in finery. He was riding a great black horse. He blew on his trumpet and he made an announcement.

"Hear ye! Hear ye! Hear ye! I have

upon this scroll a message from the king."

Ti-Jean and his parents came into the yard to listen. They'd never seen a herald. They'd never heard a message from the king in all their lives. The herald blew on his trumpet again.

"Hear ye! Hear ye! Hear ye! Let any man who has knowledge of a secret belonging to the princess come to stand before the king's throne. He who speaks the secret well and truly will win her hand in marriage. Hear ye! Hear ye! Hear ye!"

Ti-Jean could hardly believe his ears. The herald rode off. Ti-Jean started dancing about all over.

"I know it! I know it! I know it!" he shouted out.

His father looked at him as if he'd gone crazy. His mother did as well.

"I know the princess's secret. I know it."

His father and mother sighed. They went into the house. They left him to shout and dance any way he wanted.

Ti-Jean didn't care. He was dressed in his work clothes. He didn't care about that either. He went running off at once. He came to the city. He came to the palace. Already there was this huge, long lineup. There were men who had come from far and near to try for the princess's hand. The lineup went round the palace three times and out of the gate.

All the men were rich. Ti-Jean could see that. They were all talking to each other. They weren't paying him any attention. He tucked himself in at the end of the line. Seemed like he was the last. Everyone else had got there faster. Everyone else had come on horseback or in carriages of their own.

Slowly, slowly the line went forward. There was more and more excitement in spite of how every minute or so there was some man coming out of the castle looking like his mother had died. Night fell. Finally, Ti-Jean was inside the palace. He could see the princess, sitting on her throne. What was left of the line of suitors was going up the long red carpet. He'd arrived. He was standing in front of her, and in front of the king as well.

The king looked as if he wanted his supper. He looked as if he certainly didn't want to be bothered with the likes of Ti-Jean.

"Just this one more," the princess pleaded.

The king rolled his eyes at Ti-Jean's ragged jacket. He sniffed in disgust over Ti-Jean's battered boots. Still, he nodded to show he was giving his consent.

"Step forward," the highest of the king's high mucky-mucks called out.

Ti-Jean went to where the mucky-muck pointed, to the bottom of the throne steps. He wanted to look at the princess, to see if she was smiling at him, but he couldn't. He couldn't seem to raise his eyes.

"Speak," said the king.

Ti-Jean gathered all his courage. "I cannot, your majesty," he replied.

"Is that not what you have come for?"

"It is, your majesty."

"Speak or depart," cried the lord high mucky-muck. "What is the princess's secret?"

"Your majesty, I believe it is private," said Ti-Jean. "It should not be spoken in front of everyone. It should not be said aloud."

At that, the princess laughed. It wasn't a mean laugh. It was a laugh of joy. When Ti-Jean heard it, his heart beat faster.

"If he were to approach, he could tell it to me alone," the princess suggested.

The king was growing hungrier and hungrier. "Let him approach the princess," he decreed.

"Come," said the princess.

Ti-Jean walked up the steps.

"Don't be afraid," said the princess.

She didn't know that his biggest fear was that this was another of his dreams. Once more he knelt down at her feet. This time, though, she bent down to him so he could whisper in her ear.

"The sun and the moon and the stars," he said to her.

"You must go to the king and tell him as well," she ordered.

Ti-Jean did that. The king nearly fainted, but the princess looked as if Ti-Jean had given her the most precious gift in all the world.

After the princess and Ti-Jean had had a chance to get to know each other more, a wonderful wedding was arranged. There was a great big feast with all sorts of delicacies and not a hint of a turnip anywhere. Ti-Jean's parents came, for sure they did. Now that he was a prince, Ti-Jean made certain they had a better life.

It's funny though. When no one in the family *had* to eat turnips any longer, they all came to realize how much they liked them. Ti-Jean had turnips put on the palace menu quite often after that.

He and the princess grew ever happier. They saw to it those piglets were looked after – one red, one green, one blue. The piglets turned into friendly, contented porkers. They were enormous. They let out oinks of delight when Ti-Jean and the princess came to visit them to scratch them behind their ears. They lived in sties like palaces. No one said anything within earshot of Ti-Jean and the princess about how pigs might possibly be used as meat. No one did anything about it either. That's how it is always, I'm supposing. There are some who win and some who lose.

I reckon you can figure out what was rude in this story and what wasn't. I reckon it's up to you.

I don't think I quite understand it.
I don't think I know what rude means.
I don't know what's wrong with my bottom,
Why I have to keep wearing my jeans.

Why can't I be more like my uncle?
Why can't I stick out my tongue
And waggle my ears at those neighbors
Who won't let me chew on their gum?

FOUR

A TALE OF RUDE TAILS

W e have to get to Weesageechuk. We do, really. It's hard to talk about him though. There's about as much use in trying to account for Weesageechuk as there is in trying to account for the sunny day that comes after the tornado that blows your house down, the pounding rain that makes you want to dance.

He even has a lot of names. Sometimes he's Nanabush, sometimes he's Nanabozho, sometimes he's Coyote.

He's holy and he's tricky, if you can understand that. I don't think I can, although I think that Native Peoples do. You might too, for all I know.

He's been with us since the beginning. He's still with us to this day. You can't even say "once" about him, not with any sense. There has to be a once though, doesn't there?

How about this then? Dogs are in the story. We'll say it was the once when dogs were dogs already. They were like today. They came in all shapes and they came in all sizes. Some had spots and some didn't; some had long hair and some had short. They all of them liked to be stroked; they all of them liked to be patted.

There was just one thing about them that was different: when two dogs met, first thing they did was look into each other's eyes and give a sort of bow.

Weesageechuk was everywhere and all over, the way he always is. He had this little tepee. There were a lot of dogs living around it. I guess you might call them a pack. Maybe they barked and kept him awake at nights. Maybe they were after him to throw sticks when he was busy. Could be he just wanted to see what would happen. He wanted to have some fun.

However it was – on that once morning – he woke up early. He went outside, he let out a whistle so the dogs would come.

The dogs didn't rush toward him, not all of them. They knew about Weesageechuk. They knew he might have something up his sleeve. Dogs don't like to miss anything though, do they? It didn't take long and they were gathered around him – some of them sitting, some of them standing, some of them pushing at his hands.

"I'm having a party for you," he told them.

The dogs were pleased when they heard that. They wagged their tails. They threw back their heads; they started barking.

Weesageechuk smiled at them. "It's for all the dog people."

All the dog people! The dogs were panting with excitement. They were bounding up and down.

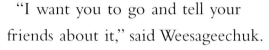

"I want you to go and tell your friends about it," said Weesageechuk.

There were dogs now licking his feet.

"When is that party?" asked the dog leader.

"It's on Friday," said Weesageechuk. "You have to hurry. You can't leave anyone out."

The dogs barked even louder.

Some ran to the east, some ran to the north, some ran to the south, some ran to the west. Some ran to places that were in-between.

"Weesageechuk's having a party," they told all the other dogs they came across. "It's just for us. It's for the dog people. There's going to be food; there's going to be drink. It's next Friday."

The dogs they met (looking into each other's eyes and bowing, mind) told more dogs – dogs who'd been scratching at fleas, dogs who'd been sleeping, dogs who'd been stretching, dogs who'd been taking themselves out for walks.

Wherever the dogs were, they all of them stopped whatever they were doing as quickly as they could manage. They all of them started running to where Weesageechuk was.

It wasn't Friday yet, but they wanted to get there early. Pretty soon there was a great big crowd. The dogs didn't know what to do with themselves, but they did know they had to be on their best behavior. They'd better not get into any fights.

Even before they started arriving, Weesageechuk had been busy. There wasn't just his tepee now. There was this brand new longhouse he'd been building. There was lots of room inside.

"That's for the party," he told them. "That's for you."

The dogs were impressed. No one had done anything like this for them for as long as they could remember.

"Now," said Weesageechuk, "I'm going hunting. You look after the longhouse. Guard it."

"We will," said the leader of the dogs. "We will."

They did too. They also talked about what Weesageechuk might be hunting for. Weesageechuk was gone a couple of days. When he came back, he had more ducks and geese and moose and deer and bear meat than any of the dogs had ever dreamed of. The dogs could hardly contain themselves.

"You wait," said Weesageechuk. "There's more."

He cooked up a pile of bannock for them to have as well. He saw to it there was plenty of water. He brought buckets and buckets. Some dogs were drooling (a few of them were sitting in puddles of drool, in fact).

Thursday night, the drummers began to arrive. They went into the longhouse to practice. The dogs could hear them. They could also hear Weesageechuk giving his orders. "This is for the dogs. You've got to be good. The dogs are important. You've got to play your best."

Friday morning, the meat was in the pots. The meat was cooking. The dogs could smell it. They started licking themselves all over to make sure they were clean. They licked their backs, they licked their paws, they licked their unmentionables. They shook themselves to get all their hairs in the right places.

Friday afternoon went by. The dogs couldn't sit still. They just couldn't. They started pacing about. Some of them were even whining.

The sun went down. The moon rose.

"All right," said Weesageechuk. "It's time."

The dogs got in a line. They arranged themselves in order, top dogs first. Weesageechuk opened the longhouse door.

"The place is new. We have to keep everything tidy," he told them. "That's why you have to leave your rear ends hanging on those pegs there by the door."

The dogs were so eager. They didn't think twice about it. They just did as they were told. They hung their rear ends up carefully, they hung them up politely, they hung them up in an orderly fashion.

There was a nice fire in the middle of the longhouse for them to warm themselves by. The meal went on for hours. There was plenty for everyone. There was plenty for leftovers, in case any dog was hungry later and needed a snack. The dogs didn't give their rear ends another thought.

"Time for the dancing," called Weesageechuk.

The drummers started drumming. Some of the dogs had never danced before. Some of them were shy.

"We can't have anyone sitting out," said Weesageechuk.

Round the fire they went in a circle, round and round and round. They did the grass dance, they did the grouse dance, they did the tea dance. They did a bit of hip hop. There was even some break dancing – doggy kind of style.

The fire burned low. Weesageechuk waited. He waited until the dogs were having such a fine old time of it they weren't paying any attention to him. He threw a great bundle of pine branches onto the embers. All of a sudden there were flames leaping up toward the smoke hole. There were flames and there were sparks.

"Fire!" Weesageechuk shouted.

The dogs were frightened.

"You've got to get out of here," Weesageechuk yelled.

The dogs went scrambling. They went running. They went to those pegs by the door. Trouble was, there were too many dogs all in one place now. They were tripping over each other.

"You've got to hurry," Weesageechuk cried.

The dogs were hurrying. They were hurrying so much they reckoned they'd sort out their rear ends later. They grabbed whichever one came to paw. Big, small – it didn't matter.

"The forest will catch fire next," Weesageechuk hollered.

The dogs went off into the night. They ran in different directions. They'd gone quite a way before they realized there wasn't a burning tree in sight. That's when they knew Weesageechuk had got one over on them. That's when they started thinking about how it would be better to have their own rear ends than the rear end that belonged to someone else.

They tried to go looking for each other, but there were so many of them and they were scattered so far. Still, they didn't give up. They looked and they looked. They're still looking. You ever notice how when dogs get together, first thing they do is have a good sniff at each other in unseemly places? Your parents will probably try to tell you it's a doggy kind of greeting. You'll know better. You'll know the dogs are on the search.

In the end, I'm not sure they came out of it all so badly. Sniffety, sniff, sniff. Wag, wag, wag. Seems to me they're kind of enjoying themselves. They might even think Weesageechuk did them a favor. Sniffety, sniff, sniff. Wag, wag, wag.

How could I be rude? Oh, how could I
When I've been to the very best schools?
I know how to walk most sedately.
I know how to follow the rules.

I know how to greet famous ladies.
I know how to lift up my hat.
To show them the frogs I've collected,
The toads and the wasps and the bats.

FIVE

ELLA AND BELLA

I know what you're counting on for this one. You're counting on another once. What kind of a person would I be if I disappointed you? Why would I even consider doing that?

Here we go then – off to the once when birds wore hats and coats and collars and ties because they hadn't any feathers yet, when lizards had to slither instead of darting because they kept tripping over their long, thin tongues.

There's nothing rude in that, I know, but surely by now you can trust I'll get to the rude part when the time feels right.

This once then – this *polite* once! – was when there were these two women. Their names were Ella and Bella. They were sisters. They lived on this farm. The farm had belonged to their parents. Ella and Bella had grown up on it. They loved it. They couldn't imagine being anywhere else.

Ella was a slip of a thing. She had skinny arms. She had skinny legs. If you stood her sideways and looked at her, you'd think she wasn't there at all.

Bella was bigger; she was stronger. She could lift sacks of

grain all day and think nothing of it. She could carry bales of hay in dozens from one field to the next.

Her strength was very useful. Ella would have been grateful if it hadn't been that Bella was always on at her, telling her if she'd just get down to it and eat more, she'd be lifting great loads too. Ella had no answer. She couldn't say anything. She did her share. She worked in the house, she worked in the garden, she worked with the animals – but they both knew Bella could do all of that as well.

Nag, nag, nag. I don't think Bella really wanted help even. She just liked gloating. The day came when Ella found she was dreading mealtime. She was thinking she'd go stark and raving mad if she heard once more about how a puff of wind would blow her away if she didn't finish the pile of meat and potatoes Bella had heaped on her plate.

"If we could have a contest and I could beat you at something, would you leave me alone?" she asked Bella at last.

"What kind of a contest?" Bella wanted to know.

"A strength kind," said Ella.

"Eat your broccoli," said Bella.

"I don't think broccoli has anything to do with what I'm thinking of," said Ella.

"And what would you be thinking of?" asked Bella.

"I'm thinking I'm a better belcher," said Ella.

Bella laughed. She pushed out her chest. She took a deep breath. She let go a good one to show her abilities. The belch that came out of her almost shook the house.

"And when will this contest be?" she demanded.

"Tomorrow," said Ella. "First thing in the morning, after we've done our chores."

"You've no hope," said Bella. "But I don't want you to embarrass yourself. I'll go to the store. I'll get you some fizzy pop."

Off she went. She brought back pop by the crate load.

Ella stacked the crates up tidily. She looked at the pop, but she didn't take even a sip. Bella went down to the basement to practice. Ella sat knitting a shawl.

"You'll need to be in bed early," Bella told her sister.

"Why would I need that?" Ella asked.

"So you can get a good rest," said Bella.

Ella kept on with her knitting. She went to bed at her normal time.

Bella went to bed too. She took some recipe books with her. She checked the ingredients for recipes like sugar pie and devil's food cake she hadn't tried on Ella yet.

Won't be much of a contest. We'll be done by lunch for certain, Bella thought.

Next morning they were both up early, having their breakfasts, doing the things that needed to be done. Bella added a few push-ups. She did them where Ella would see her.

Ella made herself a cup of tea. She went to sit on the porch steps so she could drink it in peace. Bella came out to her. She had a dozen or so pop bottles under each arm. She set them down where Ella could reach them.

"Is this where the contest's to be?" Bella asked.

Ella nodded. Bella sat beside her. She let go another one for good measure. The sound of it made Ella's ears ring. She thought she'd be deaf for a week.

"Are we competing for the loudest belch?" Bella asked.

"No," said Ella. "We're not."

"What *are* we competing for then?" said Bella.

"We're competing for the belch that can do the most – the one that has the most power to it," Ella replied.

Bella wasn't expecting that answer. Not that she was worried. She wasn't worried at all. She crooked her right arm. She made her muscles bulge. She stood up. She did a few knee bends. She sat down again.

"You could go first," she suggested.

"I'd rather you did," Ella replied.

Bella crooked her left arm. She made the muscles bulge there as well.

"Remember what you have to do if I win," said Ella.

"I do remember," said Bella.

"I want you to promise," said Ella.

"I promise," said Bella. "Would you like me to open a bottle of pop for you to drink while I'm starting us off?"

Ella shook her head.

I'll go for something spectacular, Bella decided. *I'll get this over and done.* She caught sight of the washing on the line. It was flapping in the wind. It was drying nicely. *Say I caused the clothespins to pop,* she thought to herself.

What came out of her was like a volcano when it's erupting. The clothespins flew off in all directions. The washing started drifting downward.

Bella gave a grin of satisfaction. *That should do it,* she told herself.

Ella thought about how she'd washed those sheets and shirts and petticoats. She considered how they'd get dirty on the ground, how they'd have to be done over. She didn't seem to open her mouth hardly. There was a sound, but it was more like a whisper.

The washing hung in the air a moment. It began raising itself back up. The clothespins came too. They set themselves back in their right places. The line was full again.

Bella was surprised, I have to tell you. "I was just getting started," she said to Ella.

Ella didn't answer.

"Is it my turn again then?" Bella asked.

"It is your turn," said Ella, "but there isn't any hurry."

Maybe that's the key, thought Bella. *Maybe I should go for long and slow.*

She took a look at the flowers in the garden. The belch that came out of her was like an earthquake when it's getting going. The roses, the daisies, the petunias started bowing down their heads.

It was the same as before. Maybe Ella had pursed her lips for

a moment. Maybe she'd swallowed. Nothing else though. The flowers looked like they'd been given a watering. They were standing up better than before.

"It's a hot day," said Bella.

"It is," said Ella.

"The heat's making me thirsty," said Bella.

"You could have a swig of the pop you bought," said Ella.

Bella downed half a bottle.

"It's warming up that matters," she told her sister.

Ella didn't say anything.

Third time will do it, Bella thought.

"I'm going for something we can't even see," she announced to Ella.

"And what might that be?" Ella asked.

"The cows in the cowshed. I'll pull their tails," said Bella.

"They won't like it," said Ella.

"I won't hurt them," said Bella. "I'll just give the tails a tweak."

You could see now she was concentrating. She was putting everything she had into it. The belch she let out didn't sound quite as loud as the others. Loud wasn't the issue though, was it?

One by one, the cows all started mooing. They were creating a ruckus.

It was only for a minute. Ella gave a little wiggle. The moos changed. It was like something lovely was happening in that shed there – a taste of summer maybe.

Ella looked satisfied. "I didn't want the milk spoiled. I sent a breeze to calm them down," she said.

Bella was getting desperate. She picked up another bottle of pop. She knocked it back. "I think I'll stand up for the next one," she declared.

Once more, Ella kept silent.

Bella belched. The tractor started.

Ella did shake her shoulders a little; she made the tractor go round the yard.

Bella opened the yard gate. Ella shut it. Bella rattled the roof tiles. Ella set them straight. Bella was red in the face; she was sweating. Ella wasn't.

Bella was going through the pop like there was no tomorrow. Ella hadn't touched it. Still, in a way, they were only even.

"We'll have to try something harder," Ella said.

Bella did her best not to look too terrified. She didn't do

much of a job of it. "Harder?" she squeaked out.

"You see that willow tree?" Ella asked.

"The one by the stream? The one that's ten minutes' walk away?"

"Do you think you could stir that willow tree up a little?"

Surely this'll be the last, thought Bella. She took a while. She gave herself time to focus. She caused the willow leaves to move some. She couldn't keep it up though.

Ella was still so cool. She was cool as a cucumber. She was cool as an ice cube. She made the willow branches whip about like there was a hurricane going through them.

"Maybe we're getting somewhere now," said Ella.

Bella's heart sank. She stopped thinking about sugar pie and devil's food cake. She knew it was probably time to throw the recipe books away completely.

"Would you like to see what I can really do?" said Ella.

She didn't wait for Bella to answer. She just went on.

"This is something I've been planning a while," said Ella. "It has to do with that shack there."

Bella was speechless. Well, no, she wasn't quite. "The one it takes an hour to get to?" she got out.

"The one that's such an eyesore."

"The one on the hilltop?"

"I'd like to get rid of it." Ella leaned forward just a little. She shook her shoulders very slightly. Her eyes lit up with excitement. "Are you ready?" she asked Bella.

Now it was Bella not uttering a word. Ella opened her

mouth a little more than she had done before, but not much. Bella saw the clothes shake on the clothesline, she saw the flowers in the garden dance, she heard the cows in the cowshed, giving their moos of happiness.

Ella started smiling. A rumble came from the tractor, the gate moved, then the roof tiles, then the branches on the willow. The bell rang on the church that was in the valley halfway between the farm and where the shack was standing. How had the church bell got into it?

The smile on Ella's face grew wider. There was a pause, with nothing happening – just sort of a movement in the far-off grass. Seemed to Bella like all the world was waiting.

There was no doubt about it. That old eyesore of a shack on the hilltop – the shack it took an hour to walk to – that shack was shaking. That shack was lifting off the ground. Higher it went and higher, all of a piece, just lifting, turning and turning, round and round.

Last thing Bella saw, the shack was no more than a dot in the sky. It was disappearing into the distance; it had gone over the horizon.

"I reckon that settles it," said Ella.

Bella had to admit that it did. By then, she'd flopped down. She was lying on her back in exhaustion. Ella went inside. She made another cup of tea. She brought one out for Bella to have. She brought some cakes and cookies to give her sister strength.

Ella went to tend to the garden. Bella had to go to bed for a week. Ella looked after her. She did everything around the farm without her — whatever it was that she could manage in the absence of Bella's strength.

Bella kept her promise. There was no more talk of Ella having to eat more than she felt like. There were a lot more salads on the menu. Ella went back to enjoying her mealtimes.

Bella knew she was beaten. She could just imagine herself getting belched over the horizon, going where the shack had gone to if she so much as mentioned Ella's diet. She didn't fancy that.

I have to say, I'm wondering whether the tale of Ella and Bella was rude enough for you or whether it wasn't. I think it should be. I think I can stop worrying about that.

I'm too old to be rude now, I'm certain.
I really can't give it a thought.
I'd much rather sit here considering
This pile of jawbreakers I've bought.

I'm planning on how I can suck them
And turn them around and around,
Then open my mouth to be showing
The wonderful colors I've found.

SIX

THE MAGIC BOTTOM FAN

I know what you're thinking. You're thinking that rude has its limits. You've got to be. People always do. They don't get it. There's rude all over – always has been, always will. There's rude and there are onces.

When was this once then? Is that what you're asking?

Brace yourselves. Get ready. It was the once when giraffes had ears so long they could be wrapped around their necks to use as scarves in cold weather. It was the once when hawks didn't soar, they scuttled. Bathtubs were all at the bottom of gardens. They weren't in sheds; they were out in the open. You can make whatever you like of that.

I'd think about it later, if I were you. We have to get on with the story.

We haven't been up to the sky people yet, now have we? That's where we're going then. We're going to the once when they wanted to build themselves a bridge. They wanted it to cross the Milky Way so they could get about and visit their relatives more easily – their second cousins twice removed and such.

They worked away at it until the bridge was almost done. There was just one more support they had to set in place. That's when they realized they'd used up all their materials. They searched high and low, all over the heavens. There was nothing. They started moaning and groaning and carrying on.

They might have gone on like that forever if it hadn't been for Mr. Cheats. He lived down below in a village. He'd never heard of the sky people. He spent all his time trying to get one over on everyone around him. His name was short for Mr. Cheats The Pants Off His Old Mother. That should give you a clue as to what he was like.

He didn't work at anything the way everyone else did. He spent all the hours he could manage gambling or practicing with his dice. A day came when he was sitting under a tree by a stream at the edge of town. He was figuring out how to roll sixes any time he wanted them. He heard a sound behind him, so he looked up. He found himself face-to-face with a nasty-looking red goblin.

"What are you doing?" the goblin asked.

Anyone else would've been terrified. Mr. Cheats started thinking about how the goblin might not know too much about gambling. He started showing him a game. The goblin didn't wait to find out what the rules were. It was the dice he was interested in. He liked the shape of them. He liked the sound they made. He grabbed them up and stuffed them in his goblin-pocket.

Mr. Cheats was angry. His aim was to come out the winner. Losing wasn't part of his plan. The goblin didn't really mean any

harm though. He offered
Mr. Cheats a fan in
payment.

"What use is a fan to
me?" Mr. Cheats
demanded.

The goblin rubbed
his hands together. He
made Mr. Cheats turn
round. Mr. Cheats heard
the fan go flap a couple of times. He felt the movement of the
air. Next thing he knew, something was happening to his posterior.
He put his hand behind him. He felt around. He knew then his
bottom was twice its normal size.

"What are you up to?" he burst out.

"I'm giving you a demonstration of what this fan can do,"
the goblin explained to him.

"I liked my bottom the way it was," Mr. Cheats insisted.

"It's all right," said the goblin. "I'm just showing you." He
turned the fan over. "This side now – the plain side – that's for
shrinking. The other side – the side with the pattern – that's for
growing," he went on.

"Well, would you shrink . . . "

"It's already done," said the goblin.

"Does the fan only work with bottoms?" Mr. Cheats
demanded.

"Only with bottoms," the goblin replied. He put the fan

down on a tree root. "You can take it or not – as you fancy. I have to go back to where I came from."

It was Mr. Cheats who was rubbing his hands together now. He picked the fan up. He stroked it. He smiled a horrible smile. The goblin went on his way. Mr. Cheats went back to the village. He sat on a bench in the village square. Soon enough, a rich old lady came by, out for her daily stroll. She was the one he'd been waiting for. Her name was Mrs. Falackerty. He pretended not to be paying her any attention. He waited until she was beginning to go by.

Mrs. Falackerty walked with a cane. She went so slowly it was easy enough for Mr. Cheats to get her with his fan. She fell to the ground. She let out a cry. She was little and she was frail, but her backside was the size of a horse now. Her servants had trouble getting her home. She took to her bed. She called all sorts of doctors.

People were afraid she'd been struck by some kind of plague. They thought any minute they'd all be getting enormous rear ends as well. There were rumors about bottoms the size of rhinoceroses or elephants.

It was only Mrs. Falackerty though. She was the only one afflicted, as they say.

Mr. Cheats went on like he knew nothing about it. He didn't say a word. He waited a week. He left her in her misery. The poor old thing was so unhappy. She'd have let in a rattlesnake if it had promised her a cure.

When Mr. Cheats showed up at her house and the servants told her he'd said he could do something for her, she didn't think about it twice.

"Bring him to me," Mrs. Falackerty told them. "Bring him to me at once."

Mr. Cheats made a great fuss about how he had to be in the room alone with her. He made her close her eyes. He said all sorts of magic words. He did all sorts of mumbo jumbo. He took the fan out from his pocket. He gave a flap to her bottom with the plain side.

"I think I might be feeling something," Mrs. Falackerty said to him.

"Keep your eyes closed," he insisted.

He did a bit more mumbo jumbo. He gave her bottom another flap. And another.

"Yes, yes," she whispered.

He made the whole show last an hour. That's how long he kept her lying there (with her eyes shut tight all the time, mind you) before he made it so she could be her own true self once more.

Mrs. Falackerty was so delighted at finding her fanny the scrimpy, boney thing it was supposed to be she got up straight away. She wrote Mr. Cheats a check for a whole lot of money. She gave him a fine meal. She said he could come to the house whenever he wanted. She told him he could walk in the garden. Mr. Cheats reckoned he'd do that. He'd do it right then.

Oh, he was pleased with himself. He strutted about among the fruits and the flowers and the fishponds. He lay down in the hammock, thinking he'd have himself a snooze. It was a hot day though, a very hot day.

He took the fan out so he could cool himself off. He didn't think anything of it. It was all right in the beginning anyway because he was only fanning his face. It went on being all right – no growing, no shrinking – until he started nodding off.

His hand slipped lower and lower. It hung over the hammock's side. It dangled there at the end of his arm. Back the fan went and forward, the side with the pattern pointing you-know-where. Mr. Cheats was getting really comfortable. He started snoring. He rolled over onto his side.

It just so happened the sky people were looking down on him. They'd been doing a lot of looking down lately, on account of being so unhappy about their unfinished project and not knowing quite how to pass the time. Mr. Cheats's bottom looked like just what they needed for their bridge. Not only that, it was rising up to meet them. Any minute they'd be able to reach out and grab it. It was that high.

It looked good too; it looked solid. It looked like it was made of the right stuff. The tallest and strongest of the sky people leaned forward. He grabbed Mr. Cheats by the bum. Mr. Cheats woke up. He yelled and hollered.

"I need all the help I can get," that tallest sky person called out to his friends.

A lot more of the sky people got in on the action. Mr. Cheats pulled as hard as he could against them. They decided they'd better tie his bottom in place. It wasn't quite the right shape, but they reckoned they could deal with that later.

"Let go of me!" Mr. Cheats shouted.

The sky people didn't. Why would they? Right then, Mr. Cheats's bottom was what they wanted most of all in all the world.

The fan, Mr. Cheats thought, *where is it?*

He remembered then it was still in his hand. He turned it over; he went to reach his bum again, to stretch his arm behind him. He was almost there. He was, he was really. The sky people gave the knots on the ropes they were using a couple of jerks. The fan fell out of his grasp.

There it was. It was drifting downward. He couldn't get it again. He couldn't. He couldn't even see it. It was gone.

That's it then. He's probably still up there, making it so the sky people can get from one part of heaven to another over the Milky Way bridge. He's probably doing it to this day. Truth to tell, he's likely more useful in the heavens – uniting families, keeping them together. He's more useful than he ever was on earth.

As for the fan, I don't know where it landed. I don't know that at all. I'd advise you to be careful if you ever happen to come upon a fan that nobody's using though. It might be in a drawer. It might be in an old antique shop. It might be on a path. Wherever it is, if it's plain on one side and patterned on the other, I wouldn't go picking it up. I wouldn't go waving it about and fanning anyone. I wouldn't go fanning myself.

So why bother with rude? So why would you
When there's lots you can do that's much worse?
Like hexing and potions and magic
And putting folks under a curse.

Like turning them all into birds' nests
To sit out in the wind and the rain
While you're dancing a waltz down below them
To show them their cries are in vain.

SEVEN

ANGELINA SPEAKS OUT

We're getting to the end. We're almost at the last story. Let's make it special then. Let's go to the once when camels didn't have their humps yet. They didn't even live in deserts. They made their homes on rooftops. They climbed up on ladders that had special rungs. They gazed at the stars and sang songs about dragons all night. People liked to listen to them; their voices were so sweet.

It's a good once because it's lovely to think about and because the girl in the story is lovely as well. It wasn't so much that she was so beautiful to look at. It was more that she was good to everyone. She spoke to people no one else would. She helped friends and she helped strangers. She never said a cross, rude word.

You'll probably think she doesn't belong in a book like this from what I'm telling you. I'd advise you to wait and see about that. I really, really would.

Angelina was her name. She lived with her father. She was his only child. Her mother was dead. Angelina wasn't married yet.

That's how it was in those days. If you were a girl, you couldn't leave home until you were.

Now it happened that a young man from another country came to the town where Angelina lived. He was taking a walk; he caught sight of her while she was stepping out the door. Right there and then, he decided he wanted to marry her. He sent a matchmaker to ask her father for her hand.

Angelina didn't know anything about it. She just knew her father was having all these meetings. That's something else that was part of those days and that place there. Marriages had nothing to do with two young people meeting and making up their own minds. Marriages were arranged by adults getting together and dreaming and scheming and working things out.

The first that Angelina heard of it, the wedding day was fixed. Her father came to tell her when she was having her breakfast.

"My daughter, you're to be married," he announced.

Angelina knew what was right and proper. She leaped up at once to run to him and put her arms around his neck.

"I'm so thankful to you, my father," she cried out.

She went on like that – being thankful – through all the wedding preparations. She helped with the lists of invitations, she stood still as could be when her dress was being fitted, she made sure everything was going to be pleasing to the guests.

Angelina's father was rich. He owned six thousand cattle. He owned all sorts of other things. The wedding went on for days. It was a great celebration. Everything was the finest. He spared no expense.

All good things come to an end, of course. At last, the wedding was over.

Angelina was waving good-bye. She was setting off for her new home with her new husband. She had to admit to herself, when she got there, that she was surprised. The house was a lot smaller than she was used to. It was a lot barer. In fact, it really didn't have much in it at all.

Angelina didn't mention any of that. She let her new husband show her around. She smiled at him. She kept on smiling as he explained to her that all he'd ever had in all the world was a hundred cattle that had been left to him by his parents.

"Where are the cattle now?" she asked him.

"I've given them to your father," he said.

"All of them?" said Angelina.

"All of them," said her husband. "A hundred cattle was what your father demanded so that the wedding might take place."

"You have nothing left?" asked Angelina.

"Nothing," said her husband.

"Were the cattle how you made your living?" said Angelina.

"Cattle are all I know about," her husband replied.

"But you have no cattle now," she reminded him.

"I'm good at milking. I'll do the milking for other people. I'll ask them to pay me for my labors," he announced.

Angelina did her best to look satisfied, and she succeeded. "You'll milk cattle and I'll keep house. I'll cook whatever you bring us," she declared.

That's how it was then, and again you have to remember – this was a time and place when men and women had different tasks. Maybe it would have been all right too, except that when people paid the husband, they mostly paid in buckets of milk. Angelina did her best with that as well, just as she'd promised. She served milk hot; she served milk cold. She served milk smooth; she served milk frothy. She used milk to make yogurt. She boiled milk down to turn it into sweets. She curdled milk and hung it in a bag to drip so sometimes they had cottage cheese.

I won't try to pretend she didn't long for something different, but did she even so much as murmur that to her husband? She did not.

Her husband had to walk quite a ways to get to all the herds he worked with. He was often gone for many, many hours. Angelina kept herself busy. When everything was done inside the house, she'd go out to sweep the yard.

Living next door there was a young man who was very handsome. He was very handsome indeed. He started to wait for her so he could talk to her. He might have been very handsome, but he wasn't very nice.

"I want you to go away with me," he told her one day.

Angelina didn't like that. Still, she didn't say she would and she didn't say she wouldn't. She didn't want to hurt his feelings. A month passed and then another, and then one more.

Her father fell to thinking he'd like to see her. He decided to pay the couple a visit, and – since he wanted to surprise them – he came unannounced. There he was then, standing on the doorstep.

Angelina ran to greet him. "How glad I am to see you, my father," she said.

She *was* glad, but she was also worried. She didn't know what she was going to give him to eat. It had to be good. It had to be something that would show him honor. Mostly it had to be meat. There was nothing in the house besides milk, as usual. She didn't even bother looking in the cupboards. She knew she wouldn't find anything there.

She and her father sat talking for a while. Angelina made him some mint tea from a plant that grew nearby. She had that at least. After a while, when they'd caught up on all the news, her father said he would like to rest from the journey.

Angelina showed him to the bedroom. She made sure he was comfortable. When she knew he was sleeping (maybe snoring even), she went outside. She paced about all over, muttering to herself. That's how upset she was.

You can guess what happened. The handsome neighbor came by. "Tell me what's bothering you," he begged her.

Angelina did. She was so troubled the words came pouring out of her. "My father has arrived. He's traveled all the way from his home to visit me. I've nothing to feed him," she said.

"What is it you need most?" her neighbor asked her.

"I need meat," she answered.

"Aah," said the neighbor. "I'll take care of that. I'll bring you meat. I'll bring meat of the finest."

"I'll give you my thanks," said Angelina.

"I'll need more than your thanks," said the neighbor. "I'll need you to remember what I told you before. It hasn't changed. I still want you to go away with me."

With that, he set off. He went to the market, grinning to himself and thinking of how Angelina would soon be living with him. He didn't just bring meat. He brought vegetables and spices.

Angelina started cooking. She started making a stew. By the

time her husband got home, the house was filled with scents such as it had never known in all the time of their marriage.

"What's happening?" he asked her.

"My father's come to visit," said Angelina. "I was so grieved I had nothing for him. Our neighbor's helped us out."

"It's good to have a neighbor who's so generous," said her husband.

Angelina went on with the cooking. Quite soon, her father woke up. He and her husband sat talking together in the living room, but I suspect they didn't talk of cattle. Her husband wouldn't have wanted to be doing that.

Meanwhile, the handsome neighbor was growing impatient. He was longing to carry Angelina off. He couldn't contain himself; he went walking by the window.

Angelina's husband knew nothing about the neighbor. Nothing!

"Come in," he called out. "You must come and join us. You must."

Oh well, thought the neighbor. In he came. He got himself introduced to Angelina's father.

"The meal is almost ready," Angelina's husband told him.

The three men talked some more. Angelina was putting the finishing touches to her work. She was also listening to them. She heard their jokes. She heard their laughter. Somehow, during all of this, she found she wasn't smiling anymore. She took the stew from the pot; she placed it on a platter. She carried the platter to the table. The three men settled themselves, all eager.

"You're fools, the lot of you," she announced.

The men were shocked.

"How could you speak to us like that?" her father demanded.

"How could I not, when it's true?" Angelina replied.

She was going to leave the room. She was going to go back to the kitchen. Her husband stopped her.

"You must at least explain to us," he told her.

"The meal is cooling," she argued.

"The meal's not important," he answered.

Angelina held her head up. "One of you is a fool because he sold something precious in return for something he didn't even need," she burst out.

She looked then at her father. His face went very red.

"You didn't need more cattle. You had six thousand," she went on.

"And yet, to get more, you traded away your only child."

Her father's face grew even redder. He had to take a drink of water.

"Go on," said Angelina's husband.

Angelina stamped her foot. "Another of you is a fool because he gave away everything he had. He gave away his means to earn a living for something he knew nothing about."

Her husband started staring at his feet.

"Why didn't you think about the future?" Angelina asked him. "You'd never done more than catch a glimpse of me. Why didn't it occur to you that a woman who wasn't going to ensure your everlasting poverty might have been a better choice?"

Her husband looked down harder.

"The third is the biggest fool of all," said Angelina.

She stamped her foot again. The neighbor was moving toward the door already.

"The third thought he could have something precious – something that was worth at least a hundred cattle! – in exchange for a piece of meat."

The neighbor was gone. They could hear his footsteps retreating in the distance. Angelina's husband and her father were looking at her. They were looking at one another.

"I'll send the cattle back as soon as I get home," her father told her. "I'll ask your forgiveness for what I've done."

"With the cattle, I'll earn us a good living," said her husband. "But I won't tell you I'm sorry I took you for my bride."

"Perhaps I'm not sorry either," said Angelina. She looked around the table. "Come," she said. "The meal is cooling. We should eat."

Eat they did too. They ate and they drank. They had a splendid meal, the three of them, and afterward they sang some songs. There were a whole lot of splendid meals in that house from that day onward. Angelina and her husband lived quite happily. She had lots of reasons to be smiling. The cattle grew in number. Her father came to visit often. There were children. The children were wonderfully well behaved.

"There's a time and a place for all things," Angelina sometimes told her children. "If you're going to be rude, make sure it's a good rude."

You can think about that. I'll leave you to it. You might find what she was saying useful. You might come to the same conclusion about what she did.

I'm right at the end, are you saying?
You're putting me in at the last,
When I'm known as the champion cusser,
When I shovel my food down so fast?

I'm finding that really insulting.
I don't think I'll be rude at all.
I think I'll just sulk in the closet.
I'll hide there and play with my ball.

EIGHT

BEWARE THE SPIRITS

Here we are. We've come to the finish. You've been wonderful, every single one of you. I can't imagine anyone I'd rather have been with.

I'm giving you a "cautionary tale" to go out on. "Cautionary" means it has a warning to it. The warning comes because I care. You might not like the sound of that. It's a bit teachy.

What if I tell you, though, that the story happened in the once when squirrels had their homes in rabbit holes, so rabbits were forced to wander from one place to another, pulling their furniture in carts behind them, looking for somewhere to live? It happened when beavers didn't beave and armadillos hadn't got into dillo-ing yet, when those things were all part of the wondrous possibilities to come.

Would you believe that now? You'd better, because if you don't you'll never get to hear the rest.

It's about this brother and sister. They were young and they were lucky. They had a grandfather living nearby. He came over every evening. He sat in the kitchen by the fire with them, telling them stories.

He told them about kings and he told them about castles; he told them about rich people and people that were poor; he told them about adventures and deeds of daring; he told them about babies being born and wild horses galloping. He told a lot of rude stories too. I'm sure he did.

The other kids in the neighborhood found out what was happening. How could they not? Every morning, the boy and the girl came out to go to school, their eyes bright and shining.

"You should hear what our grandfather told us," they'd say.

Trouble was, they were teasing. The other kids begged. The other kids pleaded.

"Tell us!" they chanted. "Tell us!"

The boy and the girl stuck their noses high in the air.

"The stories are for us. He's our grandfather," they'd answer.

Nothing, nothing, NOTHING would get them to change their minds. The other kids gave up after a while. That might have been the end of it, except the other kids weren't the only ones who were unhappy. The stories were as well.

The stories knew it was their job to be passed on, to be

carried to other times and places. They knew they were supposed to be making people laugh and cry and shiver and scream all over. They knew they were being put out of work.

The stories had spirits. Because that boy and that girl were so mean and so mingy, those spirits were shut in a bag. It was a sack kind of a bag. It hung in a horrible, dark corner in the basement. The fabric was smelly and itchy. The spirits were overcrowded. There were dozens of them in there, and more were appearing every night.

The spirits kept hoping that the boy and the girl would relent, but they didn't. They wouldn't! No way!

The day came when the spirits couldn't stand it any longer. They started complaining to one another. Their voices got louder and louder.

The grandfather had come over to borrow a saw. He'd gone down into the basement. He heard the stories' voices. It took him a while to figure out where the sounds were coming from, but he managed it. He knew something bad was being talked about, so he crept closer to find out what.

By then, the spirits were getting even angrier. There was a lot of ranting.

"What do they think they're up to?"

"How dare they?"

"Keeping us imprisoned."

"Keeping us trapped here."

Next thing the grandfather knew, the spirits were going on about how they were going to take revenge.

"I'll turn myself into a stone," said one. "I'll stand in that boy's way. I'll make him fall and hurt himself. I might even make him break his leg."

"I'll go for the girl," said another. "I'll magic myself into that candy she likes to buy herself. I'll make it taste so bitter it might be poison, for all she knows."

"When will you do it?" asked a third.

"Tomorrow," the first two answered. "Why should we wait any longer? Haven't we put up with enough?"

"We'll get them when they're going to school," a fourth one added.

A great chorus of shouting went up. Turned out, the stories were going to make all sorts of other things happen. The boy and the girl were going to find themselves up to their necks in mud puddles. They were going to have rocks fall on their heads. They were going to be tricked into drinking water that would make them sick.

The grandfather was horrified. The next morning, he got up extra early. He walked to school with his grandchildren, taking another route. It was longer, so they whined and fussed about it. The grandfather took no notice. He came after school too. He made them walk back by the same path.

That night, instead of telling them stories, he took them down to the basement and showed them the bag. They could see it was writhing and twisting. They wanted to run away, but the grandfather wouldn't let them. In fact, he gave the bag a squeeze.

A dreadful roar of fury came out of it. There was a lot of shouting as well. The boy and the girl were terrified. The grandfather made them listen. He was pretty mad at them himself. He couldn't imagine how his grandchildren could be so nasty and so mean.

The spirits were grumbling and rumbling about how they'd been cheated in their plans.

"Do you recognize any voices?" the grandfather asked his grandchildren.

The boy and the girl had to admit they knew all the voices they were hearing. They knew them very well.

The voice that was talking about turning itself into a stone – that one belonged to a prince, a good prince. The voice that was going on about the candy that might have been poison – she was a brave, brave girl. The voice talking about mud puddles – that was the old lady who owned the magic wand, the one who had helped a poor young lad through a flaming forest.

The boy and the girl looked at each other in panic. They knew right then and there they were going to have to change their ways. Luckily, the next day was a Saturday. Out they went, first thing in the morning.

"We're going to tell stories," they shouted. "We want you all to come."

At first no one did. The other kids thought they were being tricked again. The boy sat down on the front steps. The girl started telling him about the queen whose children turned into swans. The kid from next door saw them at it. That kid came and sat down as well. When the swan story was finished, the boy began on how the world came to be made out of an island on the back of a turtle. Another kid sneaked up and another. Seems to me there was a tale of two women who got into a belching contest next. There might also have been one about three little pigs that were different colors, and maybe one about a woman who should've been dead. I can't be certain about that. I just know that before long, there was a great big crowd of kids gathered, and they were all of them having the time of their lives.

"We could do this every Saturday," the boy said.

"You have to promise to pass the stories on though," the girl put in.

That evening, their grandfather asked them, "Would you like a new story or an old one?"

"Something the others will want to hear as well," they answered.

The grandfather smiled.

I'm happy to report that that was it for the bag. They went to check it the next day. It was silent, and it was empty.

"I don't think this will be needed any longer," said the grandfather. "I think we can throw it away."

You can probably guess why I'm telling you all this. It's because I don't want any spirits in bags where you're living. I want to be sure the stories are safe with you. I want to be sure you're safe with them.

Off you go then. Start wherever you feel like. Rude stories or polite ones. It doesn't matter. Even if you only tell one story to one person. As long as you do that, you'll be fine.

There, that feels better. I can relax now. I can put my feet up. I can stop worrying. I can listen to a few more stories myself.

Should I make this good-bye a rude one?
Or should I make certain it's nice?
Should I bow, should I scrape most genteelly?
Should I put in a touch more spice?

If I stood on my head, would that do it?
If I cavorted and gamboled and flew?
If I decked myself out in long ribbons
And painted my earflaps bright blue?

A NOTE ON SOURCES

MR. MOSQUITO. From *Gypsy Folktales* by Diane Tong (New York: Harcourt Brace Jovanovich, 1989).

THE SKELETON IN THE ROCKING CHAIR. This comes from a story I heard Toronto storyteller Norman Perrin tell to celebrate the life of yet another teller – Murray Garrett. Norman's version came from a picture book by Cynthia C. DeFelice entitled *The Dancing Skeleton*. This in turn was adapted from "Daid Aaron II" in *The Doctor to the Dead: Grotesque Legends and Folk Tales of Old Charleston* by John Bennett (Columbia, SC: University of Carolina, 1995). I made the skeleton into the wife rather than the husband because that seemed to suit my telling better.

A RED ONE, A GREEN ONE, AND A BLUE ONE. From "Ti-Jean and His Three Little Pigs" contributed by Franco-Ontarian teller Camille Perron (aka Pépère Cam) in *Next Teller: A Book of Canadian Storytelling* collected by Dan Yashinsky (Charlottetown, PEI: Ragweed Press, 1994).

A TALE OF RUDE TAILS. I heard this story told many, many times by Odawa elder Wilfrid Peltier. I am aware that there is much controversy over who may tell First Nations stories, but Wilfrid always insisted his stories were to be shared widely, and I honor that. You can find more information about Wilfrid by researching under the other variant spellings of his two names: Wilfred and Pelletier.

ELLA AND BELLA. This one's my own. It was inspired by a bush tale I heard from teller Ed Miller at a story swap in Canberra, Australia. That too was about a contest, although I seem to remember it involved sheepdogs or flies (or maybe both). I loved the slow build to the climax, remembered a friend who told me how she and her brothers and sisters had dynamited a shack during their childhood, and I was away.

THE MAGIC BOTTOM FAN. From *The Sea Of Gold And Other Tales from Japan* by Yoshiko Uchida (Berkeley, CA: Creative Arts Book Company, 1988). The story there is called "The Tengu's Magic Nose Fan," so you can guess the adaptation I made.

ANGELINA SPEAKS OUT. From "A Woman for a Hundred Cattle" in *Fearless Girls, Wise Women & Beloved Sisters: Heroines in Folktales from Around the World* by Kathleen Ragan (New York: W. W. Norton & Company, 1998). The story is Swahili in origin.

BEWARE THE SPIRITS. From *The Tale of the Spiteful Spirits: A Kampuchean Folk Tale* by Carole Tate (New York: Peter Bedrick Books, 1991).